Come Along, Daisy!

JANE SIMMONS

SCHOLASTIC INC.

New York   Toronto   London   Auckland   Sydney
Mexico City   New Delhi   Hong Kong

To my mum
—J. S.

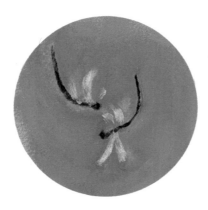

ISBN 0-439-18846-6

12 11 10 9 8 7 6 5 4 3 2 1   9/9 0 1 2 3 4/0

Printed in the U.S.A.   14

First Scholastic printing, September 1999

"You must stay close, Daisy,"
said Mama Duck.
"I'll try," said Daisy.

But Daisy didn't.
"Come along, Daisy!"
called Mama Duck.

But Daisy was watching the fish.

"Come along, Daisy!" shouted
Mama Duck again.
But Daisy was far away,
chasing dragonflies.

"Come here, Daisy!" shouted Mama Duck.
But Daisy was bouncing on the lily pads.
Bouncy, bouncy, bouncy.
Bong, bong!

Plop! went a frog.
"Quack," said Daisy.
"Ribbit," said the frog.

Bong, plop!

Bong, plop!

Bong, plop!

Splash!

"Quack!" said Daisy, but
the frog had gone.
"Mama," called Daisy, but
Mama Duck had gone.
Daisy was all alone.

Something big stirred underneath her.
Daisy shivered.

She scrambled up onto the riverbank.
Then something screeched in the sky
above!

So Daisy hid in the reeds.
If only Mama Duck were here!

Something was
rustling along the
riverbank.
Daisy could hear
it getting closer . . .

. . . and closer,
and closer,
and
CLOSER . . .

It was Mama!
"Daisy, come along!" she said.
And Daisy did.

And even though Daisy played
with the butterflies . . .

she stayed very close to Mama Duck.